GHOST WALK

Native American Tales
of the Spirit

Written by Gerald Hausman
Illustrated by Sid Hausman

A Mariposa Book

Published by
Mariposa Publishing
922 Baca Street
Santa Fe, New Mexico 87501
(505) 988-5582

FIRST EDITION 1991
SECOND PRINTING 1994

ISBN 0-933553-07-02

for Joe and Janice

TABLE OF CONTENTS

Little Bear
Canyon

oren hiked into the Gila on a full moon night in August, following switchbacks where they cut the canyon. Four miles into the basin, where the Little Bear River ran between the vertical walls of stone, he made his camp. There the pine trees looked burnt in the moonlight, as if a forest fire had come into the canyon and torn them apart, first one direction, then another. Satisfied that he'd found a perfect campsite, Loren sat down on a poncho that he spread out on the sand. He looked back the way he had come. High on the canyon's rim, he saw the rock marker his grandfather had told him about. It looked like a bear cub. In the notch between the burned-out pines, with the moon coming up full behind it, the little bear

9

looked almost real.

When he was a young boy and his grandfather was still alive, the old man had told him about this place. How he had wandered into it on a trip with some friends. Far away from Navajoland, there was something here that reminded the old man of his youth. He had spent a week wandering in the canyon. He often spoke fondly of that time.

Loren remembered how his grandfather's face shone when he came home after that trip. And the old man would never tell what it was he had seen there or what had happened, only that he had washed his hair in the traditional way; that he had camped by the river and watched the moon rise in back of the stone bear. This was all that Loren knew, but it was a lot. He had carried the image of his grandfather, the bear, and the rising moon in his mind all these years. So that now, after arriving in perhaps the very spot where his grandfather had pitched his own camp, Loren felt satisfied.

He fell asleep like that—sitting up, leaning against his backpack. And he dreamed. In the dream, he saw his grandfather washing his hair, in the old way, with yucca root. The old man was pounding the roots, scrubbing his hair with the thin suds, pouring cold water on his head from an old Army canteen. Then he sat in the sun and combed his hair with his fingers. He was old in the dream,

but he had raven's hair, black as lightning.

    When Loren woke, he felt the warm sun on his eyelids. It was mid-morning, maybe ten o'clock. In the cottonwoods on the other side of the river, Loren heard parrots screaming. He chuckled, thinking that his friends back home wouldn't believe him if he told them there were tropical birds living in a desert canyon. But he knew how they had come up from Mexico; he had read about it in the newspaper. Ever since the nineteen thirties, when they were almost extinct, the birds had been coming to this canyon in the Gila. His grandfather had brought only one thing back from his trip here: a blue-green parrot feather.

Listening to the birds quarreling in the leaves, Loren remembered his dream. Once again he saw his grandfather pounding the yucca root by the river. Then he reached up and felt his own hair, which was matted and stiff from the sweaty hike into the canyon. Loren smiled to himself. Though he was not yet twenty, his hair had already begun to turn white. This had started to happen when he was only in the sixth grade. Back then, it had frightened him and he had his mother help him to dye it black.

But his mother explained to him that it was natural—some young men of the tribe had "wise hair." The legend said that Nuthatch had come along and sprinkled wisdom on the heads of the people, and this was how they got white hair among the black.

In the canyon sitting by the river, he wondered if it were true: things done in the traditional way bringing tradition into a man's life. Entering high school, he had stopped dying his hair black, even though some of his classmates refered to him as "the old man." Now, listening to the parrots make their hoarse cackles in the tree branches, the thought came to him, gently and persuasively. First he saw the yucca plant in the loose rock alongside the cliff. Then he got up and climbed up by the stunted oak and cholla, and dug the yucca out with his hands. The loose rock and sandy soil made it easy to find the hidden white root.

Pounding the root to make suds was the hard part. You could pound all day and get only a few suds. But as he began the long, slow process, he felt good about it. It joined him to the dream he had, which joined him to his grandfather. And there was the canyon itself, a part of the dream, a part of his grandfather, now a part of himself.

When the yucca's soap was sticky on his hair, he put his head into the cold river and opened his eyes underwater. Then he rubbed on more yucca, root-bark and all, sudsing again the way grandfather used to do.

By the time Loren's hair was dry, it was late morning. The noisy parrots had flown off to quieter, cooler coves by the river. Here, by mid-afteroon, the sun was loud and hot, and there was no cover. Loren went for a swim, came out refreshed, lay in the sun and fell asleep almost immediately. When he woke this time he knew he had not dreamed. His skin, when he touched it, burned. He had lain out too long and gotten a sunburn. There was nothing to do but make supper.

By the time he'd gathered juniper sticks for the fire, the sun was setting on the canyon's rim. Loren had not spoken a word all day and he wondered how his voice would sound in the dry, empty air of the canyon. Singing a soft whispery chant as he fried bacon in a skillet, he listened to himself. His song and the sputtering grease matched in intensity and purpose. He smiled. Loren liked being alone, and though he often felt lonely when he was by himself, the feeling itself was not bad; it was how you thought about it.

After eating a bacon and egg sandwich, he lay back on his poncho and listened to the wind in the cottonwoods. There was a thrum as a string makes when it is tightened. This was the canyon sighing, expelling air at close of day. Soon it would grow quiet again. Then, in the morning, the wind would start up, moving in the opposite direction, drawing air into the canyon. Like the breathing of a person, Loren thought. The canyon was a living presence, a being unto itself.

When darkness came and the intermittent noises of owl and cricket gave new life to the canyon, Loren rose and went for a walk. At first it was a desultory meander into the upland country on the other side of the river. But the longer he walked, the more he felt a yearning to find something. Perhaps it was brought on by the memory of his grandfather's parrot feather. Perhaps not. In any case, he stumbled in shadow, wondering—half-way up the canyon wall—why he had come so far.

Somewhere, deep in the canyon's belly, his campfire smoke mingled with the last breath of wind. But he was deep in the chaparral of stunted oak and gnarled cactus. Little leaves caught in his hair, which he had bound in a ponytail. He felt the heavy weight of his hair bob behind him, coming to rest between his shoulder blades.

I think grandfather would've laughed, Loren thought. For he sensed that he was lost.

This made him laugh out loud. Laughing for his grandfather and himself. "Lost," he shouted out into the darkness. And the echo turned around and came back and made him feel very foolish. Then he sat down on a rock. Grandfather always said, he thought to himself, when you're confused it's because your mind hasn't quite caught up with your body. So Loren sat down and gave some thought to the fact that he was lost. He had gotten himself somewhere up canyon, he knew that—But where?

The undergrowth was too dense to pierce with his eye, and there were no familiar landmarks. After a time the moon came up over the rim, and though he couldn't see it, the coyotes told him about it. Their song was the rising of the moon.

Then his eye rested upon a kind of hole in a boulder not twenty feet in front of him. In the surrounding dark, the hole in the rock looked even darker.

Loren got up and went over to look at it. It was big

enough for a man to squeeze into—immediately he wondered what lay on the other side of it. Without thinking, he began to pull himself through the opening in the stone. Once inside, it felt as if a human being had scored the rock all around with some kind of blunt tool. Dry oak leaves crackled as he crawled over them.

Once through the hole, he saw something amazing. He was standing in a little hollow, a place completely sheltered by the overbite of rock and the windbreak of oak and pine. It was like a secret room in an ancient house. Hidden away like it was, Loren wondered if he were perhaps the first person to find it.

The moonlight lay like snow in the tiny walled room. Lovely and quiet, the place spoke only of peace. Yet every so often, there came the call of the far away owl, reminding him that the canyon, immense and fathomless, waited on the other side of the hole he had just crawled through.

Standing in the room made him feel awkward, so he sat in the sand. Looking down, Loren recognized a mano and metate; the cup-shaped stone and pounding tool used for grinding corn. Quickly, he stood up—the hair on the back of his head felt as if a centipede were walking there.

Once again, he looked at the stone walls of the little room. His presence seemed intrusive and he wanted to leave. But just as he felt this, he saw the loom-ties hanging from the northern wall. Someone, Loren thought, a woman, had strung the ties to the wall in order to weave a blanket. There were knobs of wood, hand-carved, where the ties were firmly secured in the stone.

He squatted down, breathing deeply.

It was then he felt himself not to be alone.

Loren sensed that someone very nearby was watching him. At first he was afraid, then he sensed that this was not an enemy. He turned around and looked all about him, but there were the white patches of moonlight and nothing else to see.

Then Loren felt the presence of something human come closer behind him. He felt it squat somewhere near his right shoulder. The centipede on his neck moved all of its feet in unison and Loren knew that his skin was crawling with fear.

In his mind, however, he kept calm, for this was his training. He said to the room: "What do you want, Grandfather?" which is the old tribal way to address a stranger.

A man's voice answered immediately, "I want to be sure that no harm comes to you."

"I am alright, sitting here," Loren told the voice. But it was an effort to keep his own voice under control.

"Yes," the voice, "you seem alright."

Then it added: "Do I know you?"

Loren answered, "I hiked in last night."

The voice was still for some time then. Loren, not knowing what to say, also kept quiet.

Then the voice said: "Would you like to have a look at me?"

"Yes," Loren said and the voice told him to turn around.

He was over by the windbreak, standing under the nut trees that grew into a twisted wall that made the place into a sanctuary.

Loren observed that he was a small man with hair cut square below the ears, and with bangs in the front of his face, like a pueblo person of today. He was short and he had the little hands of a child, and the round face and large bright eyes. He was not wearing very much clothing, just a breech-cloth which hung well-past his knees.

"I am no longer one of the people," the little man said sadly.

Loren nodded.

The man laughed once, then fell silent.

"Can you tell . . . that I am not one of the people anymore? . . ."

"—Your skin," Loren answered, "it is almost transparent."

He laughed a short whistly laugh.

"Can you see all the way through me?" he asked.

"Not quite."

"What is it like?"

Loren, still standing, shifted from one foot to another.

". . . like looking through the leaves of a tree when the sun shines through them," he said.

But this did not approximate the hesitant shape of the little man who seemed to float on waves of moonlit air, to appear both bold and uncertain, as if his existence depended on the moon, the wind, the stone room without a roof.

He seemed satisfied with Loren's answer.

"Have a look around," he offered, his presence

flickering with transmuted life.

    Loren looked around as much to be polite as anything else. But as he looked, he saw something—a woman kneeling by the loom-ties, grinding corn. A child, a girl playing with a cornhusk doll. They paid no attention to Loren. And he felt, then, as if he were the ghost and they, the flesh-and-blood counterparts of himself. Perhaps, in this canyon room, the reverse of life's usual equation were true.

"Do not try to pick up anything that you see lying about our home," the little man said. "Leave the bullrush mats, the black waterjars, the grinding tools. These belong only to us."

Loren explained that he had no desire to touch anything that did not belong to him.

"For that I thank you," the man said.

Then he added, "Do you know the reason I am here?"

Loren replied that he did not.

The man smiled and came closer to where Loren was standing.

"Do you wish to know why?" he asked.

"Yes," Loren said, "I would like to know."

Loren and the man sat, cross-legged, a couple yards away from each other.

"I want to tell you what happened here," he began. "Then you will understand."

"—Something that happened here in this place?"

"In the canyon below. You see, a long time ago there was a great flood. I was one of the Watchers. My work was to tell the others when the waters rose half-way up the canyon wall, so we could move to safety. But I was young and foolish. The night I was supposed to be on watch, I was hunting turkey. When I got back to where our village used to be, the water had carried away everything. The only family that survived the flood was my own. There were five of us left. We stayed here, alone. It was terribly lonely. I could not forget that I was the one who had abandoned our people. Because of that they were gone. And we were alone.

"The years went by. In time, the others died of old age. I, alone, lived. I was the last of our tribe. I lived here, just as you see it now. Deer were plentiful, the cattails by the river, tall and sweet. But I was completely alone. Sometimes I saw hunters come into the canyon, but always they went out the way they came. And I was alone again.

"The years went by and I grew old and one day, I died."

He seemed to be through talking. Loren waited a while, then asked how it was that he looked so young.

The little man snorted, his face full of humor.

"I am what you see," he said. "That and nothing more."

Loren said nothing. For there was nothing to say.

"As I told you, I am a Watcher," he added. "You were lost so I helped you to see the entrance of our home."

For the first time Loren thought it odd—talking like this with a ghost, a man who had lived and died, and yet was so much like himself, each of them sitting cross-legged in the moonlight.

"I believe I can find my way now," Loren said.

But when he stood up, the little man was gone. He felt stiff from sitting still so long.

Then Loren gave the secret room one last look; it was empty, the loom-ties hanging in the windless air. He looked for the woman and the child, but they were nowhere to be seen. Then he crawled back through the hole in the rock and hiked down the canyon to the river. There was a sense of harmony in the way he climbed, the

direction his feet took. Somehow he knew that he would not be lost again.

When Loren got to the sandy place where his bedroll was tucked under the box elder tree, he looked up at the canyon rim. The moon had only just found the bear cub.

This meant he had actually been gone from the

basin only a few minutes.

He lay down on his bedroll.

The box elder bugs crawled over his arms and legs and wandered across his face. Loren made no movement to brush them off. Instead he lay there, attending only to the moon as it crossed over the head of the bear cub and rose in the sky to fill the entire canyon with radiant light.

It was then he saw the feather, sticking up out of the sand, as if it had landed there from above. A blue green parrot's feather. He rubbed it against his face, gently shooing the box elder bugs on their way.

From a great distance an owl hooted three long hoots into the white night.

Rain
Runner

ne hour before the 10 kilometer
cross country race, Rain Runner
saw the hawk, her brother, fly
overhead.

Now, she was running
through the middle distance of
the race. There were three Ute
men and one Navajo just behind her. She didn't know
how close they were, but she could hear their almost
unison breathing.

They were close.

But she would not, due to her training, permit the
luxury of looking back and seeing them, seeing where
they were, in reference to where she was. This was a race
of the heart across country she knew by heart—her own
Navajo country—and it was an open race in which any-

one could participate who was over eighteen years of age.

As she ran, evenly and low, bending into the wind that was coming at her from behind and giving her an edge, she heard her grandmother laugh.

—Ha, ho, ha, ho—

She blinked to chase the phantom thought from her mind. But like all phantom things, it would not leave until it was ready.

Didn't one of the Hero Twins, sacred deities of the Navajo, the offspring of the Sun Himself, run such a race as this? Her grandmother's face flitted like a moth before her vision. Yes, it was so . . . the softer brother, the womanlike one who was known as Born of Water. He had

been chased by a band of Utes. That was why her grandmother came into it; for she had told Rain of this story when she was starting out as a runner.

The real Ute braves in back of her did not want to be beaten by a woman. They pressed on, hard. She felt them in the neck hairs where fear lived. These men wanted a victory, an old, old enmity satisfied—a triumph over the Navajo.

Opening up her stride, she began to pull from deep within the tension and tissue, the madness and hurt and love that was herself. A hammer struck at her chest and took her breath away. Fire flamed in the bellows of her lungs. The face of her grandmother, the story of Born of

Water, all these things flowed within her.

Now she was moving like her namesake, the wind sweeping her up and taking her with it. The hawk-wing wind. Here, over the sage-spotted plain that was her home, she did not think she could be beaten. Going over the lava beds her people called the Blood of the Giant, she counseled herself to slow down. Running too hard this soon could cost her the race. Remember, her coach used to say, "Run with the heart and the head."

Run flat, she told herself, let your feet fall like drops of rain.

As soon as she said this, she felt the first true raindrops strike her forehead. Good, she said, this is the way I like it, with the hawk and the rain.

But she could still feel the thrust of the Ute men at her back. They were strong distance runners, mountain-bred and trained, and they were not going to give up without a fight. Somehow, even as she pushed harder up the gradual ascent, she knew they were gaining on her. One had pulled out in front of the others; and her Navajo brother in the race had fallen far behind and she could not feel his support any longer.

Rain saw the sky darken. Her face was lashed with tears, but there was no salt in them because they were sky-fallen and driven. She wet her dry lips with them.

The country changed again. They were out of the

sage flats into the mesa lands. The trail was tightly carved out of red clay ravines. Twice she banged her elbows as she pumped upward, trying to gain speed on the incline. In the calves and quads, she began to experience the first onset of depletion. Once, before she could correct it, she sagged against the crumbly walls of the ravine, and some dirt went down the back of her singlet.

They were in the country of the owl now. Rain knew the story well; how Born of Water was taken in by Owl Brother and hidden from his enemies, made invisible by white light. Otter Brother had taken him in too, and Brother Ground Squirrel. Rain laughed, remembering how her grandmother used to sometimes change the animal genders to please her little granddaughter. The way the old stories were told, it was always Brother instead of Sister. But Rain's grandmother believed that Born of Water was slim and clever like a girl and not as hard and masculine as his brother. So she made the animals into sisters.

Suddenly the desert dark sky was shot with blue. The clouds, crimson and torn, dropped away. Out came the sun, white and hot and it burned the rainwater in the small of Rain's back. She glanced up above in the hope of seeing a hawk, but there was none. The empty vault of heaven held no mystery, no message for her.

So she ran on.

Ever more steep, the trail became a scar in the gleaming schist that spangled in the sun. Now the sweat on her face mingled with the raindrops in her hair. She tasted the two tastes on her tongue, the salt and the sweet. But these sensations were fading, now, in the dread fall-out of her agonized brain. Rain's breath came in gulps, shorter and shorter grabbings of oxygen, of which there did not seem to be enough.

She'd dropped low and light in the knees to keep up her pace, but gaining the altitude of the mesa top was taking all the strength she possessed; there was no trickery anymore, no mental or physical games that would employ her deeper spirit.

Rain did not know it, but she was on automatic. Her body had defeated the dialogue between her nerves and sinews, her heart and head—she was now on her

own, in the true fearless ether of the race. A place of no beginning and no end.

She was not aware of the sleek dark runner who had occupied a position just in back of her left elbow. Nor did she feel him overtake her as she came out into the final open stretch toward the San Juan River. Across that, and she was home free. But she did not think of it.

A fine glitter of golden rain came from the cloudless dome of blue. The San Juan was the color of coffee when it boils; the river edges white with milky froth.

The cross country ribbon sticks had fallen, minutes before the sudden storm, into the galloping river, and now they were gone. Nevertheless, the Ute man hit the water in full stride. He was a good length in front of Rain, and a good head taller. Lean and rangy, he seemed evil, the one who gloats over winning and stalks off into the sun.

But Rain did not really see him.

She felt, instead, her legs go out from under her as the claws entered her back, cutting into her flesh and raising her into the air.

Looking up, she recognized the dark shroud of hawk feathers, but the head was higher than the sky and she could only see the yellow point of the beak, glinting in the sun.

Below, the San Juan churned like turbulent coffee-

milk. Rain thought she saw her feet dancing on the surface, but she couldn't be sure.

Then the gravel of the shore and the silvery runnel of spray coming off her legs as she hit the last length of shallow water. The dark of the sun had passed, the talons sprung from her shoulder muscles. She was free and clear on the other side of the river. The white strip of winner's tape lay before her.

She collapsed into it and felt the feathers rise over her head, brush her hair with one great awkward buffeting.

The tips of the wings made a sound of shearing the air.

And Rain dropped into that sound, feeling as she fell that her chest had been seized up and carried away into a deathless place that killed memory and mind, but left the heart beating like a captured thing that tries to break free of its captor.

The heart pounding, near unto death. The circles of her hawk sister like a black corona around the sun, gave knowledge that she was alive. That she had beaten the Ute warrior. That her grandmother and Born of Water were proud.

That she was Rain . . .

Rain.

Runner.

Dream
Walkers

im Tom was sitting in English class listening to the teacher talk about plural nouns. His notebook was open and he was pretending to be interested in what she was saying, but his mind was elsewhere.

"I'll give you plural nouns," Jim Tom said to himself. He wrote the word cow fifty times, in fifty different ways all over the blue-lined sheet of notebook paper.

Cows, plural. Cow, singular.

So simple, any fool could get it. Then why did he—and half of his class—say corns, when they meant to say, corn?

He stared out the window. The land was flat. Blues, greys, browns. Plurals. Different values of colored sand.

Could you say sands? You could, couldn't you? What a funny language, English. Jim Tom thought that he might never understand it.

He wondered if language, if words, dictated how people in different parts of the world actually thought about things . . .

He wondered if people, his people, the Navajo thought a certain way because of the words they used . . . or didn't use.

He wondered.

Then his daydream carried him far off into the back country of his mind, places where his teacher, carrying her grammar book, would be completely lost. Places where he, Jim Tom, was completely at home.

Once, when he was five, his grandmother had showed him the hogan where a witch was supposed to live. From that time on, whenever he saw the hogan, he thought about the witch, who was said to be a man with great dark power, a man that you left alone. When he was twelve, Jim Tom and his brother, Caleb, who was thirteen at the time, and much wiser, watched the old witch man chopping wood. They had crept behind a big rock, and they peeked around it and watched him chop.

They were disappointed because the man chopping wood chopped like any other man. He breathed the way other men breathe when they are exerting themselves.

He paused and rested his back and wiped the sweat from his forehead just like wood-choppers everywhere on the reservation.

The other sad thing for Jim and Caleb was that the man who was said to be a witch looked no different than other men. True, he was old, his hair was white. But other than that, he was perfectly normal. Jim and Caleb went home and they soon forgot the old witch who was probably not a witch at all.

The year Jim Tom turned fifteen, he and his brother were out on the mesa with their twenty-two rifle hunting ground squirrels.

They stayed late, long into the afternoon.

As they were preparing to leave, a cow came out of the brush, and scared them. Without thinking, Caleb, who had the rifle cradled on his arm, raised the gun and fired a shot. One bullet. But that one bullet went through the cow's right eye and killed it.

When the cow rolled over and died, Caleb let out a gasp. Right away, they saw what a stupid thing Caleb had done.

Now the sun was a rim of fire on the horizon and the wind at end of day picked up and whistled on the ridge.

"—What do we do now?" Jim Tom said in a shattered voice.

"Well, we can't let all this meat go to waste."

"Are you saying we should butcher it?"

"Yes. And we better work fast, too."

"No one's going to see us in the dark . . ."

They worked side by side, using the sheath knives they carried with them when they went hunting together. Caleb was the expert—as he was in everything the two of them did. Jim Tom merely followed his example. They had plenty of experience doing practical work, and while a cow was bigger than a sheep, their experience with butchering sheep was extensive. The meat was cut into portable chunks and then they rigged a travois out of the wet cowskin.

They were a sight—covered with blood. But they couldn't see themselves, so it was just as well. It took several trips to haul the meat down the mesa, but they worked quietly and efficiently, and in a couple hours it was done.

"Now what do we do?" Jim Tom asked.

"We give it away," Caleb said.

"How?" Jim Tom wanted to know.

His brother furrowed his brow. Then a thought came to him.

"Follow me," he said with authority.

So the two boys put the meat on doorsteps in front of trailers and hogans and houses around where they lived. Dragging it from house to house took more time than they had expected. At last it was done. The really strange thing was that no dogs barked when they came up to deliver the meat. No doors opened. It was as if the world were asleep and they were dreamwalkers on some secret and mysterious errand.

When it was done, Caleb turned to Jim Tom with a worried look on his face.

"What's the matter with you?" Jim Tom asked.

"I just remembered who was the owner of that cow—"

"—Not the old witch man . . ."

"That's the one."

They both looked each other in the eyes. Then the old relaxed look came back into Caleb's face, and he smiled his confident smile.

"He's not a witch, anyway," he said knowingly.

Jim Tom wasn't so sure.

"If you don't give a witch his due," he said, his voice trembling, "he can kill you—just like that!"

Caleb snorted scornfully.

Then he picked up the cowskin—all that was left of the butchering—and wrapped the heavy blood-dripping thing over his shoulders. He danced with it wrapped around him and the cow's head wobbled when he walked. It sat on the crown of his head and the blood spattered down into his eyes. Jim Tom watched his brother shuffle in the sand.

"We'll give the old man his due," Caleb moaned.

Jim Tom didn't have to ask to know what he meant. What his brother was going to do was deliver that miserable hide to the old man.

"Don't do it."

But Caleb was already running off in the direction of the old man's hogan. Jim Tom, being an accomplice, had nothing to do but follow. In his heart, he knew it was wrong. . . as wrong as killing the cow in the first place.

The hogan of the witch was set apart in a little valley surrounded by high sand hills. It was all by itself. To get to it, you had to walk down in plain sight of the hogan. Nor was there anywhere to hide when you got there. Just the hogan, the door to the hogan, facing east, and the

red sand dunes all around.

Caleb ventured down the dunes, walking almost proudly to show how unafraid he was. Jim Tom walked behind him. On the way he saw something fearful—a lightning-struck tree. Bad sign, his grandmother used to say. In the cloudy moonlight, Caleb danced forth wearing the bloodskin of the murdered cow.

When they got to the hogan, however, even Caleb paused to consider what he was doing. Looking around him, he saw the depth of their isolation. If anything should happen here, no one would know about it. The silence was penetrating. A low wind scratched along the dunes like a crippled lizard. Little skittering noises came and

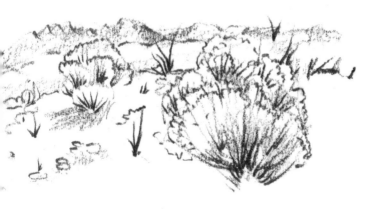

went, and with them, the wind would come and go.

Caleb seemed poised at the doorway of eternity. His right fist forever suspended for that fateful knock.

Then Jim Tom felt something touch the skin on the back of his neck. It felt like the whisper of a juniper bough. That scratchy sweatery feeling that both itches and hurts at the same time. Whirling around—he observed there was nothing there but night—so much of it and so little of him. He wanted, then, to stop his brother with a cry, but it was too late. Caleb had already pounded and the echo of his fist thudding the plank door rang in both of their ears.

At first nothing happened.

Then the door swung wide on its rawhide hinges.

As he looked inside, Caleb's voice, sounding as if it were coming from somewhere deep in a well, shouted out a gasp of surprise. Jim Tom jumped a foot in the air, and started to run. Then Caleb threw off the cowskin and he too turned and ran for the steep dunes that lay behind them.

They ran through the dark and the wind.

In back of them was the hogan, with its door ajar.

The wind, the dark.

The red diamond dunes, sparkling in the moon.

They ran without speaking, taking reedy breaths in short gasps. Their footfalls landed hard on the sandy

earth. That and their nearly unison breathing were the only sounds that came out of the darkness. It was a mile or more to their own house—a silver trailer with a hogan out back—but they made it in record time.

Jim Tom was first to get to the standing water pipe which lay between the hogan and the trailer. He knew what to do. Strip down fast and crank on the icy water. The blood was everywhere, matted into eyebrows and hair, stuck like mud on the cheeks.

Then it was Caleb's turn. While his older brother

splashed himself clean, Jim Tom shivered and shook himself into his jeans and shirt.

Neither boy said anything about what they had
seen or heard; what had happened back at the old witch
man's hogan. That was sealed and put away: Now they
must, somehow, find a way into the trailer without dis-
turbing their grandmother, whom they knew would be
sitting in her favorite rocker in front of the television set,
which was facing the front door.

There was no way in or out without being seen,
they knew that. They also knew that their grandmother
would be waiting, waiting as the moon waits on the hill
for the first wail of the coyote. There was no getting out
of what they were in, they knew that too.

"We'll walk in and say nothing," Caleb said bravely.

"She'll spot the whole thing right off," Jim Tom
said, cleaning his ear with his finger.

Caleb shook his hair like a wet dog.

"Hey, quit that," his brother said.

"Well, I don't suppose you've got a better idea—"
Jim Tom started to walk for the trailer.

Caleb caught up with him.

"—Well, do you?" he whispered menacingly.

Jim Tom said nothing. There was a ringing in his
ears. He felt dizzy, but he didn't want his brother to
know about it. So he kept walking straight for the front

door of the trailer.

When he got to it, he opened the wheezy screen door, carefully. Then, without looking back, he took a deep breath and walked in.

Caleb, somewhat deflated by his brother's forcefulness, followed quietly.

Inside, it was as they imagined.

The old lady was in her rocker with a Mexican shawl wrapped around her. The lights were off and the

television was on, splashing the walls with grey-blue eruptions. The sound was turned low, almost off. The old lady was snoring into the televison set, her head propped forward on her hand, as if she were about to say something.

Jim Tom and Caleb walked by, single-file in their bloody clothes.

Instantly, the snoring stopped.

The boys froze in their tracks.

The snoring resumed. They walked on into their bedroom.

Undressing in the dark, they got into bed without saying a word.

They were quiet for a minute before Caleb said confidently: "She never saw a thing. . ."

"Want to bet?"

Silence.

Thoughtful silence. Two minds working like mill-wheels.

"—Did you see it?" Caleb asked, his voice tremulous and soft.

Jim Tom nodded in the darkness, then added: "mmhmm."

More thoughtful silence. Nearby, a dog howled. Followed by a cacophony of coyotes. Then the reverse. The voices of the superior dogs adding adamancy to their coarse, high-toned preaching. Then the coyotes trailed off with a kind of mocking laughter.

Again the profound silence filled the room, setting the boys farther and farther apart, until they were almost like separate planets in a distant universe, each floating in a gravitational pull of thought that excluded the other.

Finally, Caleb said: "I'm sorry, Jim Tom."

"It's okay."

The voice sounded whipped, completely done in.

"If I hadn't of—"

"If grandmother had wheels, she'd be a bus," Jim Tom answered smartly.

"Hey, I told you that one."

Jim Tom whispered back, "Do you think. . ."

But he didn't finish.

"Do I think, what?" Caleb said, raising his voice.

"Not so loud," Jim Tom whispered.

Both boys knew what it was that Jim Tom was trying to say, and yet neither one tried to start the talk up again. Instead they lay in their separate beds, separate worlds, dreaming wakefully of the face at the old man's door that was not human.

"I musn't fall asleep, I musn't fall asleep—"

"And why musn't you fall asleep," the young teacher with the round eyes and black wire-rimmed glasses, said.

Jim Tom opened his own eyes wide.

He recognized the place, the classroom. He had fallen asleep in the classroom. The teacher had dismissed English class. He was alone with his teacher and her face was inches away from his. He could feel her probing his mind the way she took apart English sentences and put them back together again.

He was not a sentence. He stood up.

"Where do you think you're going, young man?" she asked stridently.

"Out," Jim Tom said.

He scooped up his books and went out the door.

Outside in the sunlight it was better. The air cleared his head. He looked around at the long low-lying shelves of desert sand, his home. The colored earth, slabs of burnt umber and brown and red. The red was blood, they had been taught by their elders. The blood of giants. Now, looking at it in the light of day, it was another kind of blood. The same kind of blood he had washed off his hands the night before.

He blinked in the noonday sun.

In front of his desert-accustomed eyes, he suddenly saw men and women tilling the soil, planting corn. They wore clothes that modern people do not wear anymore; these were the Old Ones. He saw them plainly where before there was only desert. They toiled in the sun before his eyes, people from another time, and their long black hair hung down and they sang as they worked, and the song rose on the bright air and was a part of the clouds, the spruces, the rocks and the corn.

He blinked again, and they were gone.

Then he went back into the school yard and walked to his locker. He was smiling. Now he knew what to do, what to say to his brother.

That night, when they went to bed and turned out the light, Jim Tom was going to tell Caleb about his vision; how it magically appeared to his eyes alone and how it vanished. He wanted to explain that this seeing into time somehow canceled the image that burned before his eyes the night before. He wanted to say that there was evil and there was good, and they lived side by side, and were brothers. But he did not say any of these things.

Just before he fell asleep, he saw the door to the old man's house open once again. Inside, in the dark, he saw the wolf. Perfectly normal, sitting with its paws folded. Then the face of the wolf turned into that of an owl, and the owl lifted out of the wolf's body and came at them with its claws flared. And then it was only the old man, coughing at them, with his voice of wind and dark, which they felt follow them all the way home.

Now he lay in bed, not talking. Soon his brother fell asleep. He could hear his deep, satisfied breathing. Perhaps he would dream, perhaps he would see the face, the

faces. Perhaps he would cry out in his sleep.

Jim Tom smiled. He saw again the bodies bent in the sun, the copper skin, the long water-black hair. He heard again the sweet rising song of the earth in harmony with the people; and the bright ears of the corn singing with the men and women as they came out of the earth. And Jim Tom knew that, whatever happened in his life, good or bad, there were the people who, like his own grandmother, came out of the earth like the corn, like the song. This would keep him, this would protect him.

And the face of darkness had no dominion in the presence of the people. And that, he knew, was why the old witch had lived alone.

His brother stirred and cried out in his sleep.

"Don't worry," Jim Tom said, comforting him, "I'm here with you."

And again he saw the shifting rows of corn flashing in the sun and he heard the song that made his people strong.

"The sun, the earth, the song,
the sun, the earth, the song. . ."

He whispered this over and over to his brother who lay quiet in the bed beside him.

Crystal Wolf

The smell of honeysuckle that came off the acacia trees beckoned Mariah to pitch her tent. The air was full of the little wooly yellow pills which were the blossoms of the acacia, and their fragrance drenched the air and made it smell like heaven. But the camping spot was a dry place, full of red ants, trapdoor spiders and alligator lizards.

By noon, the sun was well above the canyon rim, suffusing the oven-like air with a rose-gold light. Mariah put down the sketchbook with the drawing of a dragonfly and walked to the river to swim. Close to the water, set like green lace, there were clumps of watercress and wild celery. All around the blue stream with its white sandy bottom there were ample bunches of cattails.

Mariah got into the water, edging an inch at a time. Above her head in the white hot air the catkins of cottonwood and ash rained down, creating an illusion of little soap bubbles glowing in the sunlight.

Half-way into the middle of the stream there was a miniature island. Mariah swam to it. In the center of the island, she discovered a flat rock on top of which were four crystal pebbles.

Something about the deliberate way the pebbles were placed, in a circle, like a snail's shell, gave her pause for thought. It was obvious someone had put them there.

Thinking about the pebbles, Mariah swam downstream. As she swam, she listened to the gargly song of the rain toads. They were everywhere, for it was mating season. Their song was thick and dreamy and it filled the riverbanks with a clatter of dark, strange, invisible life that came from the earth and water and sky.

Swimming in the primeval sound, she rolled onto her back and watched the catkins come down. It was a place, she reminded herself, where the soul was born anew.

Later on, when she was toweling herself dry on the bank, Mariah saw a dark-skinned Havasupai sawing a log by the side of the river.

"Hello," she said.

He nodded, but did not answer.

The man was handsome, in a dark way. But there was something of the canyon in him that frightened her, took her breath away, like the feeling she had entering the cold water of the stream.

For a brief time, they exchanged glances. His was a straight-to-the-heart, unashamed stare, seeming to go through her, or rather, not looking at her at all. Hers was tentative and quick, that of a swallow darting from a branch. Covering herself with the towel, she walked to the comparative safety of her tent.

As she walked by him, she saw that he had a hard-boned muscular face, handsomely formed, but dark as the rock that walled the canyon and kept it from the outside world. He had shoulder-length hair, styled in dreadlock fashion. She reached the entrance of the tent and turned around because she felt the man was staring at her. To her surprise, she found that he wasn't there at all. The half-sawn log was there, gold and grey in the sun. But the man was gone.

That night, after supper, Mariah remembered the flat rock on the little island. She had an irrepressible urge

to see it again. So she ran down to the stream and waded out to where the spit of land stuck out of the water. The flat rock was there, but there were only two pebbles of quartz. They were in the center of the stone. All around her, the rain toads roared with their unabated mating song.

Night came slow. Like a great hunting cougar, it walked down out of the highland hills, perched on the canyon rim, and late, very late, pounced down into the depths of the canyon, filling the place with silence and mystery.

By then, Mariah was in her sleeping bag, trying to fall asleep. It was still hot, the rocks giving off their warmth

in waves that wafted into the tent and made her sweat. Finally, she got out of the damp bag, and lay on top of it, with the tent flap open to the breeze, which came in little puffs from the breathing of the stream.

It was the middle of the night before she finally fell asleep. And it was much later than that when, bold and unannounced, the wolf entered the tent, putting its paws on her leg.

Mariah jumped out of sleep, and stifled a scream with her fist—for the wolf was inches away from her, its silver eyes boring into her own. Growling, it eyed her. Then its mouth fell open, she saw its teeth gleam in the dark, and it turned and bounded out of the tent.

She heard its feet on the dry leaves, then pishpash, it went into the stream, pausing at the island to shake itself dry.

Fascinated, she watched the big animal, pushing at the rock with its paws. Then it bounded to the opposite bank, its hind feet splashing, and was gone in the night.

Needless to say, she slept not a wink. She did not lie down either. She sat up all night, watching. Towards dawn, she dropped off to sleep. She slept like that, sitting up in a cross-legged position, her head folded against her collarbone like a bird.

It was shortly before the middle of day when she awoke, covered with sweat. The tent was hotter than a bread-oven. Mariah got up and, wearing only a t-shirt, went down to the stream to bathe. Naturally, she swam out to the little island.

The flat rock was there.

But the pebbles were gone.

The day, crazy with heat, passed like any other. A burning hot, honeysuckle-scented, wild celery-tainted, blue sky day. However, unlike all the other spring days in the canyon, this one was oppressively quiet.

The rain toads, it seemed, had taken the day off.

Mariah listened for them long into the dreary afternoon. But they never began. The woods rang in the stillness, an eerie, preternatural quiet. Even the canyon wrens, always weaving their skirl of blue-note scale, were not to be heard.

The canyon was quiet. And it seemed that all things in it, including Mariah, were subdued.

That night, as usual, Mariah filled her canteen at the stream's edge. Night was coming on in the traditional way—the topmost walls of the canyon still aglow, the lower walls grey and gloomy. She walked into the stream, as far as the island. The flat rock was in place, but there were no pebbles on it.

Once in her tent for the night, she vowed to stay awake and watch for the wolf. Sleep, however, overtook her quite suddenly, and when she woke up out of a dream-

less sleep, the morning heat was already upon the tent. Quickly, she ran down to the stream, threw some water into her face, and waded out to the island.

The quartz pebbles were still not there.

Then the idea came to her that she was supposed to move her tent, that she was not wanted there . . . perhaps that was what the wolf had been trying to tell her. After all, it could have hurt her, if it had wanted to.

By noon, she had packed up and moved her tent to the east side of the river. There she sat, idly drawing, until nightfall. Then she made a late supper and sat outside in the starlight. A playful breeze came up the canyon and danced in the leaves of the ash trees.

When she awoke, startled by a sudden sound, she discovered that she had fallen asleep, leaning against a sapling. The silver-eyed wolf was sitting at her feet, head resting on its paws.

Mariah's heart gave a start, jumping in her chest. The wolf raised its white-brown face, its attentive starlit eyes drawn to her intake of breath. Yet, this time, it did not seem angry with her. Its eyes were no longer cold or accusatory. She watched as it deliberately stood up, stretching, then moved leisurely downstream to where the little island shone in the shivering starlight. The wolf waded into the water, hopped onto the island, did something with its paws, and bounded away into the woods on the opposite bank.

She watched the white flag of tail flash, vanish.

Then, like engines everywhere, all around her, the rain toads began their singing. A clatterous soundtrack of noise filled the banks of the stream. At the same time, cool air began to flow between the tree trunks.

Mariah listened, almost gratefully, to the scattered poppings of the rain toads. The night chirped and chortled, grated and groaned. And the cool, soft canyon air fed the hot rock-walled place with the breath of spring. Minutes before, it had been dead summer. Now it was the season before, the time of the rain toads.

In the morning, Mariah went out to the island. There were quartz pebbles, dozens of them, in concentric circles like the shell of a snail.

It was an odd feeling she felt then. A feeling of intense discovery—as if all that she now knew precluded everything else. Now, there was this thing that she understood. It had to do with the toads, the pebbles, the wolf, the canyon. She knew little else. Nor was anything else important.

That night, when the wolf came into her tent, she was not afraid. With her heart, she welcomed it. The wolf's fur had grown black, thick and dark. Its paws had grown soft as the spring air, not calloused, and its breath was sweet as wild celery. She felt it lick her, just once, and she reached out for it, but it was gone. Her arms closed upon the empty air.

Mariah cried softly in her sleep for the rest of the night. In the morning, when she woke, her eyes were red-rimmed and heavy, and she knew that the time had come for her to leave the canyon and go elsewhere.

On the way out, later in the day, she stopped at the community bulletin board in the village of Havasu. The mule train had come in with a week's worth of mail. The air was full of the commotion of dust and dogs. The canvas panniers of boxes from the world outside the canyon were being unloaded by strong stout Havasu women. There was the dust and the light, the white, wet mules, the women busy about their silent, thankful task.

Mariah watched as a woman with waist length hair hefted a big carton into the tribal community center. The way she walked, slow like the night. The way she held the box, soft like a child. The way she looked, once, into Mariah's eyes.

Mariah looked around the village square. There was nothing else. The peach trees were growing their

green nubby fruit. The children were playing in the shadows under the trees.

On the bulletin board, she saw a message scrawled in a big loose hand. It said, "Whites will give up digging for uranium only when mother earth's heart stops beating." Below the message was a wolf's paw print in red, green, gold and black.

Mariah studied the message and the symbol below it for a long time. When she finished looking at it, the mule train was going up the trail ahead of her.

Time to go, she said to herself sadly.

Time to leave my home.

On the way up the switchbacks, leading out of the Grand Canyon, she sang herself the song of going away, the song of leaving lovers and friends and lives that are lost behind canyon walls.

"The stars," she sang, "are the windows of the flowers and the flowers are the windows of the stones; I am the window of myself and my pleasure is the gateway of the corn."

Armed only with a song, she left the canyon.

Perhaps he will follow me, she thought.

But she knew he would not.

Zahgotah

hester Jim was a tracker. If you asked him what he liked to do more than anything else, he would say, "I like to track animals." And that was what he did, whenever he had a chance. But it was not how he made his living.

He earned his daily bread as a janitor at the Canyon County Day School. Tracking animals was not profitable, so Chester did it as a hobby. Nevertheless, he was said to be the best tracker on the Mescalero Reservation. Everyone knew he could find a hummingbird's nest in a summer sandstorm. Chester knew it too. So it didn't make much difference to him if he swept floors, washed boards, and emptied baskets for a living.

One weekend as he was packing some things in a knapsack and preparing to go off on one of his personal tracking expeditions, a man on a spotted horse rode up to his little shack.

The man was a friend of his, someone he'd known since high school.

He didn't bother to dismount. With the sun behind his head, his long hair hanging down, shoulder-length, he looked like an Apache from a long time ago. The fact that he was wearing running shoes and a red baseball cap somehow did not alter the image. He had a heavy face, small, narrow, wolflike eyes, and an unusually long jaw. He was built like an adobe brick.

"Goin' off," he said to Chester.

Chester tightened the straps on his old-fashioned Boy Scout knapsack, a present from his father more than thirty years before. It looked new, the leather straps and the silver-alloy buckles were oiled and polished. Chester stuffed some elk jerky into the pack and hefted it easily to one shoulder. There he shifted his weight to the hand that held the pack, and looked into the quiet eyes of his friend.

He said nothing.

"Dry summer," the rider said, creaking forward in the saddle.

"Yeah," Chester said. Then, "What'd you want,

Lee, I'm on my way out."

"Wonder if you mind doin' us a favor. . ."

From years of experience with his people, the questioning with eyes rather than words, Chester knew what was being asked of him; and also who was doing the asking. The tribal council was still out searching for Zahgotah, the man they called The Enchanted Apache. No one could find him. Lee Lazytree had been delegated by the council to ask Chester to give it another try.

"I don't know," Chester said hazily, scratching his forehead. "Zahgotah's been missing almost six months."

"His wife's asked us to try one more time."

Lee untangled his horse's mane from under the bridle strap that separated the horse's ears. A wasp caused the horse to sidestep just as Lee fingered the tangled mane, but he leaned with the sudden shift as if nothing had happened.

Chester smiled at his friend's agility. He was no horseman, himself. He was, his father had told him, one of a long line of oldtime Apache stalkers, men who prided themselves on footwork. He could walk all day and not get tired. He could walk all night and sleep standing up if he had to, and often when he didn't, just for the fun of it.

"—Well, what's it going to be, Chess—"

Chester squinted into the sun; he had less than half

a day of tracking left. Zahgotah was gone, but he wasn't going to say this to Lee because he knew that Lee knew it as well as he did. It wasn't something to say, that was all. What they both knew, they didn't need to say. This, out of respect for the widow, for that was what she was, already, a woman without a husband.

"I'll be talking to you," Chester said, and turned to head into the back country behind his shack.

"We'll be waitin' on you," Lee Lazytree said softly as he watched his friend slip like a two-legged snake into the cottonwood shadow.

As he walked along, feeling the hot dry sunlight across his shoulders and the good solid weight of the old knapsack sitting squarely between his shoulder blades, Chester thought about the missing man named Zahgotah.

He remembered the morning, two months back, when, chasing a good-sized bear, he found himself studying the footprints in the mud. You know how the back feet of a bear look: like a man's bare footprint, only with

claws. The claws make a difference, but there are times when tracking bear, you get the sensation you are tracking a man.

Of course, a bear and a man move in totally different ways. They naturally have opposite styles of movement—one looks deep into things, and is more cautious than the other. You can see this in the print itself, the way it meshes with the earth.

Chester remembered that morning, in October, that he was tracking a bear that moved a little too much like a man. He had thought, at the time, "maybe this bear's eaten some fermented apple and gotten himself so drunk he thinks he's a man." But then a thing happened that he would never forget.

The bear tracks suddenly turned into a man's. The man was wearing cowboy boots. There were four sets of prints and they crossed in and out of each other. There were the bear's and the man's, and then nothing but the man's boot heels.

Then the boot heels wandered off a little ways and disappeared.

Chester studied the prints for an hour or more. He'd never seen anything like it. Finally, he accepted it for

what it was; something he didn't quite understand. The conclusion was good enough for him. Good enough for government work, his friends used to say.

That's the way things were out in canyon country. You didn't always have an explanation for the way things were. Nor did you try to force one out of the emptiness, the mysteriousness of life. You let it be. And you went on with your business. But there were those who saw prints just like these, and some of them made a fuss over it. A hundred men on horseback saw tracks just like the ones Chester saw. And they claimed they recognized the spirit that made them.

Zahgotah.

They said they saw a whirlwind come up out of the sand and blow dust into their eyes. In the dust and the

wind, they saw the shape of a man. The shadow of a man wearing white Tony Lama cowboy boots. When the wind let up, he was gone. The only thing left of him were the white cowboy boots with the silver tips. These were in the center of the circle of horsemen. Nobody would go near them.

Then the reverend over at White River did a sermon on that piece of work. He said it was the devil playing tricks, trying to make bad men out of good ones.

"It wasn't Zahgotah," the reverend said. "Now you all know that was a poor little man, out of work most of the time, and you know what that does to a man. You know he was an epileptic . . . he couldn't dance in a dust-wind or scale a cliff like a cat, and even though there's people say they saw him do these things, we know better, don't we?"

But what about the time in Badger Canyon, Chester wondered. Some tribal policeman swore they saw Zahgotah dancing around on a cliff, wearing the white Tony Lama boots that he left everywhere, and that nobody would touch. Jake Shonto claimed that he saw Zahgotah dance like a goat on the edge of the cliff. He and his friends were sitting around their campfire, talking and listening to gospel music. Someone said: Well, I bet old Zahgotah would like to hear some of this music . . . too bad he's dead . . . ."

And when Jake went to turn the radio up a little louder, he looked up and there was Zahgotah, dancing. He said he looked like a mountain goat. But some of the other guys said he looked more like a coyote. One said his nose was longer than it had ever been while he was alive. But it was him; they each swore to that.

After that, everybody started seeing Zahgotah. There were people who saw him in Cibecue and Hon Dah on the same day. Everyone knows those towns are far apart. But a man at a feed store in Cibecue swore he saw Zahgotah crouching over a spoiled grain sack. Said the man was eating bad grain, stuffing it in his mouth, swallowing it down. Said the fellow's shirt sleeves were trailing in the dirt and his forearms were covered with long dark-black hair. Same day, people over at Hon Dah claimed Zahgotah was seen pitching horseshoes with a bunch of schoolkids and they said his front teeth were little like a housecat's.

Then the whole tribe went out on a massive search and rescue because there were people who believed Zahgotah was still alive. Chester thought back on his involvement in all this. What Chester had said, publicly, was this: "What are you going to do if you find him? You can't arrest a man for going away into the wilderness . . . you can't put him in a hospital if he doesn't want to go . . .you can't send out a posse for a man who hasn't broken a single law. . ."

But who ever listened to reason when there was cause not to? There must've been hundreds of trackers from all over the state, just looking for Zahgotah. It got to be a regular off-season sport. It was a long hot summer, and no rain. The search parties were falling all over themselves, and there were hunters bragging about getting off 'sound shots' whenever something moved in the bushes.

No one knew what Zahgotah was living on—if, in fact, he were alive at all. Some said he lived on juniper berries, wild grass and chokecherry bark. Some said they found evidence that he ate raw deer meat, but they were

the same trackers who said they saw him show up at a dance one night.

The story went that Zahgotah showed up in those white Tony Lamas. He danced the night to dawn—this same man who was an epileptic. Around sunrise a girl named Beverly Longbow went home and on the way she saw Zahgotah sitting by a large bear cub. She said he and the bear were polishing his boots. The bear would lick them with its tongue and Zahgotah would rub the silver tips of the boots on the bear's neck fur to polish them.

Beatrice Zah, Zahgotah's widow, said the first words she ever heard him speak were these: "I will be back tomorrow." This was when she first met him, twenty years earlier. He didn't return for several years that first time. Later on, after he'd disappeared last summer, she got scared and locked her doors and windows. "They told me he had turned into something," she said, "I got real scared."

Beatrice said she put holy oil on her front door every night. She'd get out her blanket and bible, and pray for her husband's deliverance. One night, she explained to some of her friends that a mountain spirit came whispering around the house. She said the spirit told her not to worry, that her man, Zahgotah, was going to get found soon.

The following day Chester found the bear tracks

that turned into bootheels.

Thinking these thoughts, wandering about the back country a few miles behind his shack, Chester came upon something that caused him to stare very closely at a young spruce tree. The score-marks on it were the kind made by a bear cub, more playful than meaningful, they indicated a happy cub having some fun. Chester sniffed at the tear in the white cotton-colored flesh of the tree. It smelled of bear. But there was another smell. Chester knew what it was—leather polish. At the base of the tree, around to the back side of it, hidden by some low limbs, he saw something whitish-looking.

Bones. White clean bones.

Chester sat there for a long time, not doing much of anything. Mostly, he thought about Zahgotah. How the people said he was a mountain spirit, a deer spirit, a goat spirit, a bear spirit. He recalled the time that Zahgotah had thrown down his Crown Dancer headdress in front of everyone. He stomped on it, denouncing the Apache religion.

That was more than ten years before he started going away and turning into things. After throwing down the headdress, Zahgotah had joined the Miracle Church, a Spanish American Baptist Revival Church in White River. He said if he was going to be cured, it would be because Jesus Christ, the savior, wanted him to be cured,

and not because some medicine man said a prayer with a pack of feathers. He was dead set against his people then, and he never really came out of it. Then he started going away. For longer and longer periods of time. First days, then weeks, then months. When he'd come back there would be a strange light in his eyes.

Maybe he just got bitten by a rattlesnake, Chester chuckled to himself. And, then again, maybe he didn't.

Maybe he went back to the hills to reclaim whatever he lost growing up on the reservation and going to Vietnam.

Maybe, maybe.

But people said he turned into something.

Maybe he had. Maybe what he turned into was not as bad as what people thought. Maybe they were all a little jealous.

Chester sat by the spruce tree for quite a long time.

He opened up his knapsack. There was a coffee thermos, and he took a long, slow drink of hot coffee, wondering why something hot made you feel cool. He took off his hiking boots and lay back, barefooted, and stared into the spruce boughs.

There was something up there. He focused on it.

The thing was white and it was moving in the wind.

Chester hardly moved at all, he just lay there, looking.

Finally, after a very long time, he figured out what was up there.

Hanging on a deerhide thong were a pair of white Tony Lama boots.

Then, all at once, Chester remembered Zahgotah's American given name. It struck him pretty funny, that name. Because, like a lot of things that didn't belong — the Miracle Church, the unemployment, the work that Apache people did because no other work was available, families not getting along and always the young ones going off to the cities where they found trouble more easily than work—the names, the American given names, didn't, they didn't ever, belong.

Chester realized that Zahgotah was one of the rare few who had beaten the rap. He'd confused just about everybody. And in the process, he'd lost his American given name.

Now no one would ever call him Humphrey again. They had even stopped calling him Zahgotah. Instead they called him the Enchanted Apache. He was a legend. And only Chester knew whether his friend was dead or alive.

Pale Ghost

After burning his suit of clothes, Hansen sat in the shade of an ash tree.

Soon, the ghosts would come. They always did.

The sweat lodge, made of mud and stone, was so hot when he stepped into it, it singed the hairs inside his nose when he tried to breathe. How did the old people do this, he asked himself, the sweat flowing in rivulets down his chest.

City-bred skin.

Soft, city hands.

City, city man.

He tapped the lava rocks with the deer antlers, moving them into place. Then he pulled the old blanket over the doorway. Immediately he was swallowed up in darkness, and the sweat of his steaming body ran into the dirt.

Prepare a place for the ghosts, and they will come...

He went outside for the third time, walked into the river, rolling like a dog in the shallows, sending minnows flying in all directions.

One more time.

For the fourth and final time, he pulled the blanket. The daylight was again sealed from him. He was in the womb of time, bathing his skin in the old life, birthing himself in the original wetness of being.

The ghosts, the parts of himself that kept him alive...

... Not there, but soon...

The sweat rolled from his cheeks, collecting in pools around his navel.

For some reason he remembered his grandfather. Maybe it was the antlers. Remembering his grandfather made him remember his grandfather's tractor, the first one ever brought into the canyon.

That was years ago, before he was born.

Brought in on mule back, one piece at a time. They thought, the other elders, that it would ruin the way things were, but it made things better. The peaches could

be harvested more easily, the earth furrowed faster. In time, everyone used the tractor.

Hansen had seen it just the other day.

Rusted-out, datura blossoms like moons, grew out of the rotten tires. Once, he remembered, when it broke down, his grandfather had put a deer skull into the hub of one of the wheels. When it broke down for the last time, after his grandfather died and he was about to go away to school in Lawrence, Kansas, he and his brother put the deer skull back in the hub. The skull still had the bullet hole that had killed the deer. The boys painted a portrait of Bob Marley on the skull, and the hole where the bullet went through was the singer's open mouth.

Now, nine years later, all of them were in the earth —the deer, the grandfather, the brother, the tractor, the singer.

Soon they would come to soothe him . . .

He sang the old song of thanks, then.

Song to the roundness of things to the beaten bracelet, the sun-shaped basket, the moon-shaped basket, the lodge made of earth, the cedar trunk, the river that wound round the earth, the stars that embraced all of them. He sang the song of first-breath, the song the river makes in the new morning when the sun is first-seen, first-felt.

Then he threw back the blanket . . .

. . . Ghosts . . .

The river cooled his hot skin. He rolled in the shallows for the last time. He came out of the cold into the hour of deception, just before evening, when shadows are being born, the time when warriors strike upon the unwary. The time when the eye is not sharp. The time when things are not separate, the lost time when things are tied together, when one thing becomes another.

He stood there in the cracking starlight and he knew that the cracks were crickets.

Crickets and stars. Stars and crickets.

Cri, cri, cri. Str, str, str.

Cristr, crstr.

Then, listening, he remembered his grandfather's tale of how as a young boy he ran one hundred and fifty miles to see the train pull into the town of Williams. He had not stopped, he had run the whole way.

The language, the old words, came back to him now in clicks and clacks, like the song of the cricket-stars. The language of ghosts. He stood by the river, dry. Hot as an ear of roasted corn, dry and songless, trying to remember more, trying to squeeze the juices of memory.

The words were like flat rocks rubbed together and they were like the rushes of yucca plaited one-over,

one-under, until, miracle—there was a basket. Words, he thought, were like this.

Ghosts...

At first he thought it was a cloud of pollen on the wind.

Grandfather?

Allen?

Tractor?

Deer?

But the ghost was all of these, a thing of permanent parts, like the tractor itself, brought in, piecemeal on mule back.

Hansen saw, quite distinctly, his grandfather. He was made of the blue pollen that rests on ponds. Out of his body came the tractor, the way it looked when it was new. And sitting on the big metal seat shaped like a leaf

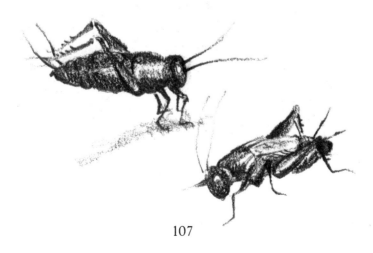

was his brother Allen, the way he looked when he was alive, before he took his life, jumping off the cliff. And the deer, bounding like a legend, sprang out of Allen's mouth.

Going down on his knees, Hansen cried.

He cried for the missing parts, for the parts that rust in the sun and rain, for the bones that do not stay, for the people that blow away.

Lastly, he cried for himself.

When he stopped crying, he looked up.

Allen was there, his skin like shining pollen.

"I have loved you like a living brother" he said.

"You are my brother, aren't you?" Hansen asked.

"Yes," Allen said, "I will always be your brother." Then: "You've called on me to tell you something?"

"Yes," Hansen cried, "what shall I do?"

"What shall you do? What you always do. That is what I have been saying all these years."

Hansen still looked uncertain.

Allen laughed gently.

When he stopped laughing, Allen was Allen again. He looked very real to Hansen. Not pollen-like. Real. A man of flesh and bone.

"You—"

"Yes," Allen said, "It is what I have been saying to you all these years."

"—are the one who is alive!"

It was Hansen, then, who dissolved, his face full of surprise.

The meeting done, Allen walked back to the village where his grandfather was waiting up for him.

He was one with his brother for another year.

Notes on the Stories

LITTLE BEAR CANYON

Loren has been a student and friend of mine for many years. His grandfather, a Jemez Pueblo elder, was the inspiration for the story "Jimmy Blue Eyes" in the book *Turtle Dream*, Mariposa, Santa Fe, 1989. Loren's lineage—Navajo and Pueblo—gives him a special way of seeing into things. The vantage point of two native cultures is strengthened by the fact that he is well-schooled in the "white way," having attended private school, and now, college. Altogether, his world-view is round, and complete.

Sometimes, however, three ways of looking at life come into conflict. I remember when I was Loren's high school English teacher. Some days he would wear his reflector glasses, sit very still, not talk to anyone. I knew, then, to leave him alone. Later, when we had a chance to talk, he expressed his indecision. There were always three or more ways to see the littlest thing. And what might seem of small consequence to someone else, to Loren, loomed threefold in magnitude.

It was in the Gila wilderness on the camping trip which the story is about, that I saw the past boil up and take him somewhere he'd not been before. We were in the canyon sensing the impalpable presences of those who had been there long ago. The place was a virtual reservoir of spirit(s).

One night Loren got lost looking for a hot spring. My daughter, Mariah, one of Loren's best friends, was staring at the full moon and saying she knew Loren was in trouble somewhere.

When he staggered into camp very late, he told us of the Watcher. I put some notes into my journal, hoping, one day, to make them into something. Next morning, and the following morning, the notes grew. The canyon, obviously, was haunted—or perhaps we were haunted, within it. In either case, Loren wasn't the only one who met the Watcher. Two other campers, Jeff and Harry, met him as well.

This happened six years ago. But today, as I write, I know that the Watcher is still there, as he has been for so many centuries, a tough little Mimbres man, living in a crack in the rock, safe in his self-made wrinkle of time. He is caught between what we call the past and the present, there, alone, to remind us that our lives, our legends go deep, deep into the earth.

RAIN RUNNER

The myth of the dark god who aids the Hero Twin of the Navajos can also be found in *Meditations With The Navajo*. In "Rain Runner" there is the fusion of myth with an actual runner. Both of these are set into the matrix of a contemporary cross-country race.

In the autumn of 1988 when I was writing a feature article on Wings of the Southwest, the national Native American running team, I discovered several runners from which to choose a heroine. I picked one and she knows who she is, but I changed her name to protect her identity.

Rain Runner, by her own admission, ran races for her tribe, for her Indianness, her tribal self. The willingness to run came from a natural, gods-given power, the belief that she was not one but many. From this was born her strength of vision. She did not see herself winning; she saw herself running. And she was not alone. She was with her people, as well as the lore of their imagery, the rich mythology of clan and kin.

The story also deals in epiphany, the gifted moment when the encumbered self is suddenly reborn. Rain Runner exemplifies this. She becomes, during her moment of winged-transcendence, not more than what she is, but *just* what she is—fully realized in the moment, a champion.

House Made of Dawn, N. Scott Momaday, Harper and Row, 1977 is recommended reading for the great running scene, the eagle-flight prose poem, the eternal theme of myth and man.

DREAM WALKERS

Certainly the theme of brothers doing right and wrong is biblical. So, too, the moment of truth coming clear in dream or vision. These universal truths are, quite naturally, an integral part of Native American mythology. (Witness the Hero Twins of the Navajo as discussed by Frank Waters in *Masked Gods, Navajo and Pueblo Ceremonialism*, Swallow/University of Ohio Press, 1990.) Sadly, this fact was tragically lost on the majority of European settlers who came to America in the centuries postdating Plymouth Rock.

My own hearing of "Dream Walkers" occurred in 1969 when two Navajos visited a school where I was teaching. One evening they told my brother and me of the secret rite of passage devised by themselves when they were teenagers: the killing of a cow and the subsequent touching of a witch or Navajo sorcerer.

In writing it twenty-two years later, I changed the story hardly at all. In fact, I found a treasure of forgotten details that were completely lost to my conscious mind. These, surprisingly, rolled out in the writing.

The friction of the two brothers is offset by the dual-dilemma of two cultures, white versus Indian. This actually gets the story going at the very beginning with Jim Tom daydreaming between two worlds, school and imagination. As the story unfolds, the tension, a kind of Cain and Abel motif, develops.

The greater symbolism of the legendary brother theme is wonderfully explicated in Waters' book. The Navajo Hero Twins are discussed as prototypes of human destiny, as well as gods. They are, in legend, the offspring of Mother Earth or Changing Woman. Their father is the Sun or Sun Father. One brother, the bold and swift, moves from the right and exemplifies the Jungian masculine principle. The other twin moves from the left and is feminine in thought and action. The Hero Twins must work together, sharing the powers inherent in each.

My rendering of this brotherly relationship includes the Hero Twin mythos, while adding to it the biblical paradigm. The writing in the story owes much to an old friend from the Navajo reservation, Jay de Groat. Jay told me about his vision of the ancient ones bending to the corn. He also acquainted me with the idea of multiple dimensions. Thus, perhaps what is called "Indian time" is a series of layers of co-existent reality. Jay would not have said it so — what need to say it at all? — But were it not for his quiet voice and vision, I might not have been able to resolve Jim Tom's moral dilemma. Jay walked in, as he has over the years, just as I was trying to complete the story. And he told me of his vision. When asked if he would like to put it into the tape recorder, he said: "And record the sound of silence?"

CRYSTAL WOLF

We have a Pueblo friend who will not permit his daughters to go to Havasu, in the Grand Canyon, unaccompanied by a family member or a medicine man. There are places that are of such strong spirit, that what is brought there magnifies and changes shape. Havasu is such a place.

It is a strange and magnificent place, a side-canyon that dwarfs all things human and yet, at the same time, brings human and trans-human into a kind of dance. Visitors often speak of voices that are lifted on the wind-current of the waterfalls. Voices that say words in old, lost languages.

Campers in the canyon speak of the eerie feeling they get near the ancient Havasupai cemetery. Sometimes climbers, striking out for the towering red walls above the cemetary, turn back for no reason. A feeling they say, an ominous feeling, says to go home.

A backpacker told me of a voice that she heard while swimming beneath a waterfall. The voice whispered "Go back!" into her ear. And she did.

I awoke one night in Havasu babbling some forgotten tongue, gesturing with my hands, standing in the starlight, appearing to speak to someone who was not there. My friend looked out of his tent and shone a light in my eyes, but I wouldn't wake up.

The story of Mariah and the crystal wolf happened pretty much as described. The incident of the wolf entering the tent actually happened to me, rather than my daughter, Mariah. But whether the wolf was a dream animal, the projection of a dreaming man, I do not know. I do know that our car was "violated" by two Indians at the same moment the wolf came into the tent. And when I yelled in my dream, the wolf ran out of the tent. Waking up, I saw a dark shadow running across the sage flats, whether man or a wolf I could not tell. Which brings us back to our Pueblo friend who does not let his daughter visit Havasu unaccompanied by a family member or a medicine man.

ZAHGOTAH

The story of Zahgotah, the enchanted Apache, originally came to me from my brother who picked it up on one of his folk-singing trips in Arizona. For years he and I have been swapping stories of Navajo witches and werewolves, Pueblo clowns and Apache demons. The old ways, the "superstitions," as they are sometimes called, are being casually, over time, lost and weeded out. The Zahgotahs are disappearing because—more than for any other reason—we do not believe in them anymore. Or we have no need to believe in them anymore. With the loss of legend, the ebbing away of belief in things not seen but felt, we, as a collective consciousness, are reduced, ciphered-down into something less.

Somehow, the Zahgotah legend found its way into the open. The story was originally told as fact, even though it sounded like fiction. I've little to add here in the way of notes except that I was personally taken, in retelling the story, by the mixture of Christian and non-Christian beliefs which crossed over each other. The Apache circumstance of poverty seemed to augment, in my mind, the fantastic nature of Zahgotah. He became a hero figure, a martyr to the old religion that, because of his own temporary loss of faith, was the cause of redemption in the pine forest. —But this happened only after he had given up his identity in the village and reunited himself with the animal people.

Zahgotah became a kind of mystic messenger, one who

comes along from time to time, urging us not to waste water in the desert. Here, he seemed to be saying, is a cup. Here, the sweet spring. See that no one spills our life's blood, Mother Earth's blessing. To accomplish what he did, Zahgotah had to leave us without word, no one knowing if he were alive or dead, real or unreal, a spirit or a fleshy form.

Zahgotah was a man of principle whose divine action, if such it may be called, was to vanish without a trace so that we would have to question or reaffirm our own faith in the great mystery that is this world. Zahgotah makes us understand, in some wordless way, that even when there is no heartbeat, there is yet the promise of life. So we must pierce the veil—or not. We must seek to understand the unknowable—or give up trying to "know" what we cannot trust to the rational mind. We must, at rock bottom, allow the suspension of disbelief and give rightful station in our everyday lives to those signs that guide us. Only then will nature, like sudden rain in the desert, nurture the hidden roots of our lives.

* * *

For readers interested in going further along the messianic vein, I recommend *Watch For Me On The Mountain*, Forrest Carter, Laurel Dell, 1983. The author was storyteller-in-council to the Cherokee nations, and the book is a kind of spiritual biography of the legendary warrior-priest, Geronimo. I thought of Geronimo while trying to get the words right to "Zahgotah." Once or twice, I wondered if the old deliverer had teased some whirlwind dust-magic back into being, sprinkling it on the head of Zahgotah, passing the power on to him so that he would tell the people it was not too late. Maybe, after unsuccessful months of trying to tell the story, Zahgotah's spirit gave my own sorry head a wise sprinkling. In any event, after many poor tries, one day, the story just bounded out of a thicket and ran in front of me.

PALE GHOST

"Pale Ghost" was told to me, in part, by a friend at Havasu. He talked about a woman who wore her hair and clothes in the "old style" and who went about offering a basket of blue corn to passersby. The way he spoke of her, she was not really a ghost. Ghosts, he explained, were what old people scared young people with. She was someone living in another dimension of time, who could, on occasion, be seen in our present time frame. When I asked if he had seen the woman, he said no. The reason, he felt, was that he wanted to see her so badly—"She only comes to those who don't care."

So who, I asked, had seen the corn-bearing woman?

He gave me a quick look and his eyes went away. And he seemed to be following the movement of the trees by the river, the wind in the air stream of the upper canyon. When he turned back to me, he said: "The only people who see her are tourists who think she is a woman from our village. Of course, once she was . . . a few hundred years ago . . ."

It occurred to me then that "ghost" is a misnomer. That is why it is not used so much by Indians. (This depends, of course, upon the tribe; Navajos use the word ghost perjoratively because, to them, ghosts are evil.) When someone dies, most Pueblo people say, "He's gone." Not, for instance, "He's dead." The word "spirit" was used often while I was at Havasu. One man I talked with said that it was foolish to try to isolate a spirit and call it a ghost when all things, dead or alive to the human eye, possessed "spirit," and hence were alive.

At Havasu the gentle winds change with the fiery or muted colors of the cliffs that go saffron and pink at eventide, then plum and dark-blue shadow, to blackest black. The moon comes out, and things turn again, and once again, as morning draws near and the moon wanes. It is not ghosts, really, but the spirit that comes back in mood and tone, in dream and vision to those who are blessed with a sixth sense, an inner eye.

Time, to paraphrase Thoreau, is the stream running down canyon. Ghosts are the little lost leaves carried away on the stream. Memory is but the blue fire of the blood that remembers the stream of time, the leaves of life gone by.

***

A beautiful story describing the parallel lines of non-linear time is Leslie Silko's "Yellow Woman" in the book *The Man To Send Rain Clouds*, edited by Kenneth Rosen, Random House, 1975. In the story myth and racial memory turn upon one another and become the same. Living in myth and living in life are not different when we realize that myth is life. In the Indian world, the word myth drops away, as do the words "religion" and "death." What remains is the indirect light of the direct present—that, and nothing more.

The Author

Gerald Hausman, poet, teacher, storyteller and editor has spent twenty-five years living in the Southwest. A former poet in residence at Connecticut State College and a resident storyteller at many colleges, private and high schools, Mr. Hausman has been a published writer since the mid-sixties. His books number twenty, most of them dealing with Native American mythology and nature. He has been awarded National Endowment and regional arts and humanities grants to teach poetry to children and young adults. He continues to teach and do storytelling on the primary, high school and college level.

In recent years, Mr. Hausman has devoted time to preserving the Native American oral tradition by recording storytellers for Sunset Productions in Santa Fe, New Mexico. Some of these recordings, including his own, have been aired on National Public Radio. Whether writing stories or telling them, Gerald Hausman believes the passage of wisdom from one generation to another is a crucial form of education.

In addition to collecting stories in the Southwestern United States, Mr. Hausman has also spent many years gathering stories in the Caribbean, particularly on the island of Jamaica where, during the summer months for the past five years, he has directed an outward bound program for high school students.

Gerald Hausman lives outside Santa Fe, New Mexico in an owner-built adobe home with his wife, Lorry and daughter, Hannah. (His older daughter, Mariah, attends college.) His pastimes are studying wildlife, running, swimming, camping and reading. This is his fourth book illustrated by his brother Sid who also happens to be his next door neighbor.

The Illustrator

Sid Hausman has lived in New Mexico for 25 years. A graduate of Highlands University, he is part of an era in which the school produced many of the renowned artists in Santa Fe today. He is known for his work in leather and jewelry, as well as music and illustration. For the past 10 years, Sid has been a resident artist with the New Mexico Arts Division, teaching songwriting at Navajo and pueblo schools including Zuni, Jemez, and Santo Domingo. In his songwriting workshops, he will often have the kids illustrate their visual interpretations of the songs.

Sid Hausman's earlier broadsides and illustrations have been published by the Giglia Press, Lawrence Hill and Co., Bear and Co., and Sunstone Press. He currently resides with his wife Cappie, in Tesuque, New Mexico.

Also from Mariposa Publishing

Children's Literature

By Joe Hayes

> **The Day It Snowed Tortillas**
> Tales from Spanish New Mexico
>
> **Coyote &**
> Native American Folk Tales
>
> **The Checker Playing Hound Dog**
> Tall Tales from
> A Southwestern Storyteller
>
> **A Heart Full of Turquoise**
> Pueblo Indian Tales
>
> **Everyone Knows Gato Pinto**
> More Tales from Spanish New Mexico

By Gerald Hausman

> **Turtle Dream**
> Collected Stories from the Hopi,
> Navajo, Pueblo, & Havasupai People

By Reed Stevens

> **Treasure of Taos**
> Tales of Northern New Mexico

Adult Literature

> **Sweet Salt, A Novel**
> By Robert Mayer

Audio cassettes and books of related interest
by Gerald Hausman

Stargazer, audio cassette, selections from the novel with additional stories about Native American contact with star people; approximately 1 hour playing time.

Navajo Nights, audio cassette, Navajo stories of healing and harmony; approximately 1 hour playing time.

Native American Animal Stories, audio cassette; approximately 1 hour playing time.

Ghost Walk, audio cassette, selections from the book; approximately 1 hour playing time.

Audio cassettes available from Sunset Productions, 369 Montezuma, #172, Santa Fe, NM 87501, (505) 471-8004.

Turtle Island Alphabet: A Lexicon of Native American Symbols and Culture; St. Martin's Press

Tunkashila: From the Birth of Turtle Island to the Blood of Wounded Knee; St. Martin's Press

The Gift of the Gila Monster; Simon and Schuster